Henry the Impatient Heron

By Donna Love

Illustrated by Christina Wald

Henry was a young heron, a Great Blue Heron that lived near a pond. His long, thin legs were great for wading, and his long, pointed bill was great for catching fish. But the young heron had a problem. He couldn't stand still.

Other herons stood still for hours, legs stiff, bodies rigid, necks poised to strike out at a fish or salamander or tasty frog that might swim by. They stood still so long that the fish and the salamanders and the frogs forgot the herons were there.

But the young heron was impatient and had been that way since he hatched. The other chicks in the rookery waited patiently in their nest high in the tree for mom or dad to return with food. Henry hopped and squawked about, too anxious to stand still.

His brother and sister said, "Stand still, you're stepping on our heads." But he couldn't.

When Henry's mother or father returned, he hopped about some more.

"Stand still," his parents pleaded, but he just couldn't. Finally, when he was so hungry he could hardly stand it, he got a little bit to eat.

It's not that he didn't try. Many times he practiced, perched on the side of his nest. But soon his legs would begin to twitch, and his neck would begin to itch. Then he'd raise his long leg to scratch his back or flap his wings to stretch. In his nest it didn't matter. His mother and father brought food, but soon he would be on his own. Soon he would have to feed himself.

When it was time to fly, the young heron liked the way the wind felt beneath his wings. He wasn't afraid. He had always lived high in a tree. With all his hopping and flapping, his large wings had grown strong.

At the pond his brother and sister stayed near his mother.

He watched a Mallard family parade by. A doe and her fawn walked to the lakeshore to take a drink. Then he spied a dragonfly and followed it through the cattails to a Red-winged Blackbird's nest.

There was so much to see and do at the pond that Henry forgot about his family . . . until his tummy began to grumble and rumble. He looked for his mother, his sister, and brother, but they were nowhere to be found. That's when he knew he was alone and would have to feed himself.

"I can do this," he thought. After all, how hard can it be to catch a fish?

He waded in the water and looked and looked. His gray head darted this way and that, watching below for a shiny fish to bolt between his skinny legs, but none did. His twisting neck and bobbing head frightened the fish away.

On the shore the little heron spotted a salamander. Oh, what a tasty treat! He could move fast when he wanted to. He ran towards the salamander with great speed, but the salamander saw him and quickly darted away. His bill hit the bank where the salamander had been, and all he got was a mouthful of sand. YUCK!

"I'm so hungry," thought the impatient heron, "I'll eat the next thing that moves." Then he spied a plump little frog sitting on a lily pad nearby.

"Just the thing," Henry thought, and he took a great big leap.

The frog jumped away just in time. Henry followed, his long legs running, wings flapping. But the frog jumped again. Henry ran smack into a log and fell backwards in the water— KER-SPLASH!

Looking up to see what he hit, the little heron saw it wasn't a log at all. It was a heron, and not just any heron. It was THE GREAT BLUE HERON, the heron of all herons.

"Oh, pardon me, sir. I thought you were a log," the little heron said with a bow.

"You are quite excused," said The Great Blue Heron, with a kingly, kindly voice. "After all, I am the King of Camouflage."

"The King of Camouflage?" the young heron asked.

"Oh yes," said the king, "I can stand still so long that even *I* think I have turned into a log."

The impatient heron hung his head and said, "I wish I could stand still. I'm so hungry I could eat a log."

The Great Blue Heron chuckled and shook his head.

"You know," he told the young heron, "when I was little, I couldn't stand still either. Then I learned the trick."

Henry peeked up hopefully and asked, "What did you do?"

With a knowing look, The Great Blue Heron said, "The trick is to look like a stick."

"Look like a stick?" the young heron asked.

"Yes," said the King. "A fish is afraid of a heron, but not afraid of a stick. When you stand very still, the fish will think your legs are sticks."

"Oh," and then Henry asked, "may I use your trick?"

"Be my guest," said the King, and off he flew with a kick and a swish.

The sun was beginning to set in the sky, but the impatient heron knew he had to try. He found an inlet that looked like a good place to catch a frog, salamander, or fish. Then he stood still and thought and thought, *I must think like a fish. I must look like a stick.*

His legs grew tired, his feet got cold, and yet, he stood quite still.

Just as the last of the light of day sank beneath the hill, a fish swam by. Without batting an eye, Henry's neck darted forward with strength all its own. When he lifted his head, a large fish squirmed in his bill.

I caught one, he thought, and then he swallowed the fish. Suddenly his stomach was quiet and full, so he flew to a perch and preened and preened, very proud of himself. When he grew tired, he put his head under a wing and happily went to sleep. The impatient heron had learned to stand still.

For Creative Minds

Great Blue Heron Facts

A Great Blue Heron's eyes are positioned on its head so it can see behind as well as from the front. A heron can focus its eyes very fast so it can search for fish at close range, then quickly switch to a long distance view to watch for predators.

When flying, herons' long necks are "s-shaped."

Herons' long necks and pointy beaks allow them to quickly spear fish or other small animals.

They can fly 20 to 30 miles an hour. Next time you are in a car, ask the driver to tell you when you are driving as fast as a heron flies.

The heron's "backward facing" knee is really its ankle and heel. Its real knee is inside its body cavity hidden inside its skin and under its feathers.

The heron has a tiny bit of webbing between two of its front toes so it won't sink into marshy ground.

When a Great Blue Heron preens, it uses its toes to scratch a patch of "powder down," a type of feather that helps insulate a bird. The tips of these feathers disintegrate into a powdery substance that Ornithologists (scientists who study birds) think may soak up water and/or be used to preen and clean feathers. When clean, it uses a "comb" on its middle front toe to straighten its feathers.

Great Blue Herons are large birds! When standing, they are approximately 4 feet tall. *How tall are you? How does that compare to a heron?*

The wingspan (from the tip of one wing to the other wing) is about 6 feet. *Use a measuring tape to see how big 6 feet is. Do you know anyone or anything that is about 6 feet tall?*

Herons are a type of bird. All birds have feathers, although not all birds fly (penguins don't). In fact, birds are the only animals that have feathers. Birds hatch from eggs, breathe air, and are warm-blooded.

Their very long legs help them to walk quietly through the shallow water.

Adult Great Blue Herons only weigh about 5 pounds. *How much do you weigh?*

How Did Henry Hunt?

Herons are carnivores. That means they eat meat. But, they don't go to a grocery store for their food; they have to find it by themselves. Herons spend most of their awake-time looking for food. If you've seen a heron, chances are that you saw it standing in shallow water, hunting.

It probably looked like it was standing still doing nothing. But it was watching very closely for prey (animals it wants to eat) to come to it. By standing still for so long, other animals (fish, salamanders, frogs, etc.) don't realize that it is a bigger animal, and they swim up to it.

The heron quickly grabs the smaller animal with its strong beak and enjoys a tasty meal.

Food for thought: wetlands

 Great Blue Herons live around wetlands all over North America from mangroves and salt marshes to freshwater swamps, lakes, and slow-moving rivers.

 What could happen to Great Blue Herons if wetlands were destroyed?

 What are some things that you and your family can do to prevent pollution in wetlands?

Heron Life Cycle Matching Activity:

See if you can put the herons' life-cycle events in order to spell the scrambled word.

G

Herons breed in large groups called colonies. They usually build big nests high in trees or on cliff edges close to water. The male gathers sticks and the female builds the nest.

T

At 10 to 12 weeks the chicks leave the nest and their parents for good.

E

The eggs hatch after 26 to 30 days.

R

Females lay between two and seven pale blue eggs. Both parents take turns sitting on the eggs to keep them warm.

A

Chicks live in the nest for about two months, and both parents feed them. That's when they take their first flight.

Answer: Great

To my father and mother-in-law, Sam and Helen Melnick, and sister-in-law, Tana, who love to watch great blue herons along the Yellowstone River near Billings, Montana—DL

To Troy for all his support and feedback and to the herons that live around his parents' house in Lake Barkley, Kentucky—CW

Thanks to Susan Bonfield, Environment for the Americas, home of International Migratory Bird Day and Cathy Wakefield, Conservation Education Coordinator, The Nature Conservancy, Mad Island Marsh Preserve for verifying the accuracy of the information in this book.

Publisher's Cataloging-In-Publication Data

Love, Donna, 1956-

Henry the impatient heron / by Donna Love ; illustrated by Christina Wald.

p. : col. ill. ; cm.

Summary: Henry the heron couldn't stand still. He was always moving, and it drove everyone crazy. All herons have to stand still to catch their food, so how would Henry ever be able to eat on his own? Henry learns a valuable lesson from the King of Camouflage, which teaches the importance of just being still. Includes "For Creative Minds" educational section.

Interest age level: 004-008.
Interest grade level: P-3.
ISBN: 978-1-934359-90-7 (hardcover)
ISBN: 978-1-607180-35-7 (pbk.)
ISBN: 978-1-607180-55-5 (English eBook)
ISBN: 978-1-607180-45-6 (Spanish eBook)

1. Herons--Juvenile fiction. 2. Birds--Juvenile fiction. 3. Patience--Juvenile fiction. 4. Birds--Fiction. 5. Patience--Fiction. I. Wald, Christina. II. Title.

PZ10.3.L68 He 2009
[E]   2008936036

Lexile Code: AD, Lexile Level: 760

Printed in China

Sylvan Dell Publishing
976 Houston Northcutt Blvd., Suite 3
Mt. Pleasant, SC 29464